The REALLY Rotten Princess

and the
Awful, Icky Election

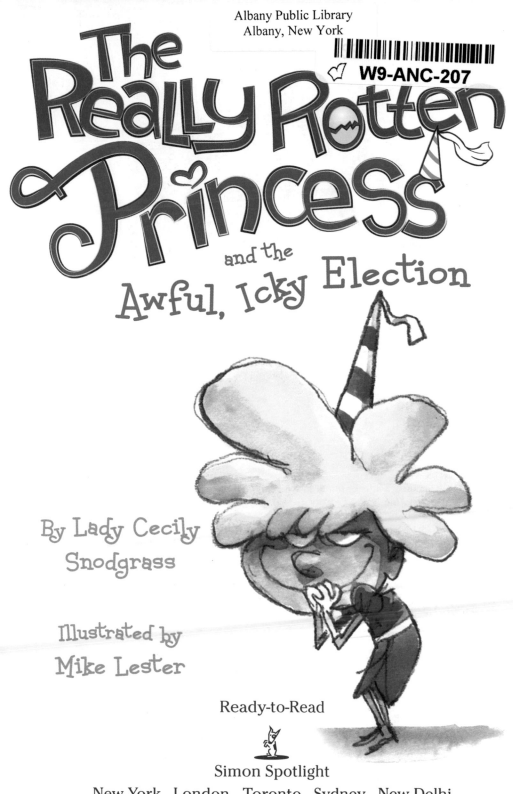

By Lady Cecily
Snodgrass

Illustrated by
Mike Lester

Ready-to-Read

Simon Spotlight

New York London Toronto Sydney New Delhi

SIMON SPOTLIGHT
An imprint of Simon & Schuster Children's Publishing Division
1230 Avenue of the Americas, New York, New York 10020
This Simon Spotlight edition August 2020
SIMON SPOTLIGHT, READY-TO-READ, and colophon are registered trademarks of
Simon & Schuster, Inc.
For information about special discounts for bulk purchases, please contact
Simon & Schuster Special Sales at 1-866-506-1949 or business@simonandschuster.com.
Manufactured in the United States of America 0720 LAK
10 9 8 7 6 5 4 3 2 1
Library of Congress Cataloging-in-Publication Data
Names: Snodgrass, Cecily, author. | Lester, Mike, illustrator.
Title: The really rotten princess and the awful, icky election / by Lady Cecily Snodgrass;
illustrated by Mike Lester. Description: New York : Simon Spotlight, 2020. | Series: Ready
to read | Audience: Ages 4-6. (provided by Simon Spotlight.) | Audience: Grades K-1.
(provided by Simon Spotlight.) | Summary: When the princesses in Miss Prunerot's class
run for president, Regina embarks on a campaign of dirty tricks.
Identifiers: LCCN 2020021399 | ISBN 9781534479289 (paperback) | ISBN 9781534479296
(hardcover) | ISBN 9781534479302 (ebook)
Subjects: | CYAC: Princesses—Fiction. | Behavior—Fiction. | Elections—Fiction. |
Schools—Fiction. | Humorous stories.
Classification: LCC PZ7.S68032 Rep 2020 | DDC [E]—dc23
LC record available at https://lccn.loc.gov/2020021399

Chapter One

Regina was still finding frosting in her hair, even after the spell that had turned her into a cupcake wore off.

But it did make her more popular
than she'd ever been before.

At least until Miss Prunerot arrived to start class.

Miss Prunerot announced that they were going to hold a class election.

THE ROYAL GUIDE
TO ELECTIONS

STEP ONE: Choose a politician

STEP TWO: Give them lots of money

STEP THREE: Try not to laugh when

they pretend they're

against you

All the princesses thought they would make the perfect class president.

But Regina was just as certain
that none of them would win.

Chapter Two

The first thing Regina did was make
a list of her own worst qualities.

There were a lot of them.

1. Hides Miss Prunerot's dentures

2. Treats servants badly

3. Plays nasty tricks

4. Plucks wings off fairies

5. Doesn't care about the planet

6. Lies constantly!!!

The next day she began
to put her list to use. . . .

For her campaign,
Princess Dragonbreath
held a big bonfire rally.

It didn't go well.

To win votes, Princess Lovelylocks
treated the class to a day
at the salon.

But someone had replaced the shampoo with real poo—bird poo!

Princess Glitterati announced that she had been endorsed by the glitter fairies!

But no one noticed that someone had sprayed glue on the fairies' wings.

Princess Litterati ended her election speech with a shower of confetti.

Princess Somnambula was too busy napping to campaign.

Regina had accused her opponents
of having most of her
worst qualities—
before they could do it to her.

All of her opponents,
that is,
except one.

Chapter Three

The race came down to
Princess Wishlicious and Regina.
It was a wild and heated campaign!

Princess Wishlicious made her closing speech.

Princess Regina made her final pitch
to just one person.

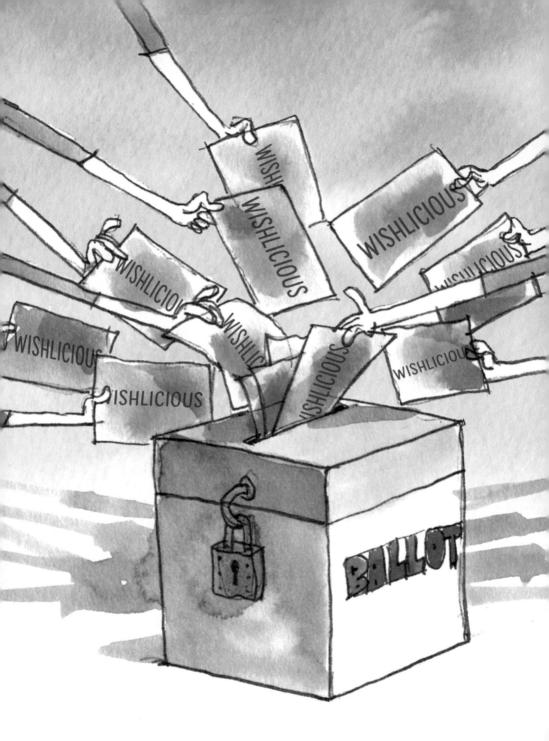

All the princesses cast their votes.

And Miss Prunerot counted them . . .

... and announced the winner.

But Regina found out that she was now under the control of the person who got her elected.

And that was just rotten. . . .
Really rotten.